Picnic Planet

'Picnic Planet'
An original concept by Alice Hemming
© Alice Hemming

Illustrated by Emma Randall

Published by MAVERICK ARTS PUBLISHING LTD
Studio 3A, City Business Centre, 6 Brighton Road,
Horsham, West Sussex, RH13 5BB
© Maverick Arts Publishing Limited March 2019
+44 (0)1403 256941

A CIP catalogue record for this book is available at the British Library.

ISBN 978-1-84886-420-7

www.maverickbooks.co.uk

This book is rated as: White Band (Guided Reading)

Picnic
Planet

By **Alice Hemming**

Illustrated by **Emma Randall**

Chapter 1

"Picnic Planet here we come!"

Spacey Stacey drove the spaceship skillfully through the stars. Her four friends sat behind her, with the picnic hamper between them. The smell of freshly baked bread was mouthwatering.

Zip and Zap lifted the lid of the hamper to take a peek at all the goodies. In the middle was a giant, orange carrot jelly from the Space Place.

"No nibbling yet – we're nearly there," said Timble.

They landed on Picnic Planet.

"It's perfect weather," said Stacey, parking the spaceship.

They piled out into the car park and gazed around. The sky was clear, the grass was blue and all three suns blazed above them.

"Where is everyone?" asked Timble. "Picnic Planet is normally packed on a beautiful day like this."

"Maybe the space bunnies put people off," said Moondoodle, pointing to the signs. "'Warning: Space Bunnies' and 'Do not feed.'"

"Who's scared of a bunch of bunnies?" laughed Zip.

"Anyway, we're not the only people here," said

Zap. Three familiar spaceships were landing on the other side of the car park.

"Oh no, it's Astro Pete and his friends," said Timble.

"Be nice," said Stacey. She waved and smiled. "Would you like to join us?" she shouted.

"No thanks," said Pete.

"No way," said Jill. "Our chocolate cake is too good to share."

"Phew," said Timble, and set off to find a picnic spot on the other side of the field.

"Look at the way the suns are sparkling on those treetops," said Moondoodle. "I'm going to go to the top of the hill and paint the view."

"What about the food?" said Zip and Zap.

"I'll only be a couple of minutes," said Moondoodle.

Chapter 2

Stacey put up a purple parasol and spread a red checked picnic blanket beneath it. They opened the hamper and laid out the tasty treats on colourful plates. Starmite sandwiches, crunchy vegetable sticks, spaceman pie, pizza and fizzy pop.

"This looks like a proper feast," said Timble.

"Moondoodle will miss lunch if she takes too long," said Zip, grabbing a handful of crisps.

"We'll call her," said Stacey. "Hang on
a minute, who's this?"

A fluffy silver rabbit with floppy ears lolloped
towards them. "Hello," said Stacey, "you're a
cute little thing. Here, have a carrot."

The rabbit took the carrot and nibbled shyly.

"The signs say not to feed the space bunnies," pointed out Timble.

"Does he look dangerous to you?" asked Stacey, laughing. She scratched the rabbit gently between the ears.

The bunny leant back on his hind legs with wide, innocent eyes.

Zip and Zap both laughed. Then, the bunny took a sudden leap forward.

BOING!

He grabbed the plate of jelly in his front paws.

"No!" cried Zip and Zap.

"Stop him!" shouted Timble.

Stacey jumped to her feet and tried to seize the rabbit, but he was too quick. He threw the jelly to another bunny, darted around her legs and disappeared into the bushes.

They all chased after the second bunny. Zip and Zap even lay on their tummies to get a better look but he had vanished.

"Well!" said Stacey. "I was looking forward to that jelly."

"Me too," said Zip.

"And me," said Zap. "At least we've got the other food."

They headed back to the picnic but Timble put his hands to his head in horror.

"The blanket!" he cried.

Chapter 3

Silver space bunnies of all sizes surrounded the picnic blanket. They lifted it clear off the ground, complete with plates, napkins and all the food. The friends got back to the hamper to see twenty white bunny tails disappearing over the hill. They could hear the space bunnies' tinny laughter.

"Is there anything left?" asked Timble.

"Nothing," said Stacey, turning the hamper upside down. "I'm so sorry, everyone."

Stacey strode over to Astro Pete, Jack Boom and Jill Zoom. They were halfway through a game of Frisbee.

"I don't suppose you guys have any food to share?" she asked. "Space bunnies just stole our entire lunch."

"Space bunnies!" laughed Jack, sticking out his front teeth and waggling his fingers above his head.

"You should have read the warnings," said Jill, pointing in the direction of the signs.

"Oh dear," said Astro Pete, smirking. He twirled the Frisbee on his forefinger. "I'm sure we must have something for you."

He threw the Frisbee to Jill, who missed it, and opened up their stylish orange cool box. Stacey's mouth watered at the sight of cheese rolls, crisps and a rich brown, chocolate cake.

"Here you go," said Pete, rummaging in the box and producing a small, plastic-wrapped bundle.

"Thanks," said Stacey sadly. She trudged back to her friends with Jack and Jill's laughter following her.

At the picnic spot she unwrapped the bundle.

"Celery?" said Zip,
"Is that it?"

"This isn't going to fill my rumbly tummy," said Zap, crunching on a stick.

Timble sighed. "We'd better head home," he said. "Let's go and tell Moondoodle."

They climbed up the hill. Stacey and Timble went ahead but Zip and Zap dragged their feet behind.

"It is beautiful," said Stacey. "I can see why Moondoodle wanted to paint up here."

"It would have been a perfect day," said Timble. "What a shame. Oh well, at least it can't get any worse."

"Let's call her," said Stacey. "Moondoodle!"

"MOOOOONDOOOODLE!" they all called.

"MOOOONDOOOODLE!"

"MOOOONDOOOOOOAAAAARGH!"

Stacey was so busy looking around her that she forgot to look at her feet.

Something gave way
beneath her and she
slipped.

Wheeeeeeee, BUMP!

Stacey suddenly
found herself in a
very dark place.

Chapter 4

"What happened?" she said, brushing herself down. "Anyone there?"

"We fell down a hole," said Timble's voice beside her.

Suddenly there was a bright light. "I always carry a torch just in case," explained Timble.

He shone the light around them and saw that they were in a space about the size of a garden

shed. They looked up. The hole looked a long way off – too far to climb out. A pair of legs dangled above them.

"Is that you, Zap?" called Stacey.

"Yes," replied Zap. "We're going to rescue you. Hold on to my legs."

"Are you sure?" asked Stacey, pulling on his foot.

"Yes," said Zap. "Zip's got my arms."

Stacey held onto Zap's legs and swung for a few seconds.

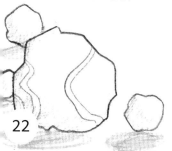

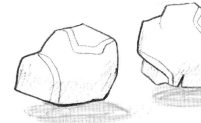

"Hang on a minute," said Timble. "What's Zip holding on to?"

A faraway voice came from outside: "A branch."

And then... SNAP, aaaaaaaaaaargh!

BUMP, BUMP, BUMP!

Zip and Zap fell into the hole, right on top of Stacey.

"Great," said Zip. "Now we're all down here. How are we going to get out?"

Timble flashed his torch into every corner of the small space. "There's a door here," he said, shining the light to the left.

Stacey rattled it. "Locked."

"There must be a way out," said Stacey. "Come on, think everyone!"

They thought.

"It's no good," said Zap. "I'm too hungry to think. And that rattling door is putting me off. Can you stop it please, Stacey?"

Stacey stood up suddenly. "It's not me! The rattling is coming from the other side. It must be a bunny. Stand back everyone – I'm going to catch one of those space bunnies and find a way out of here."

She stood beside the doorframe, ready to catch a bunny. The door swung open, and Stacey pounced.

"Come here, you pesky bunny!" she yelled, grabbing it.

"Aargh!" said the bunny, in an unbunny-like voice. "I'm not a pesky bunny: I'm Moondoodle!"

Stacey let go and sat up.

"Moondoodle!" cried everyone. "How did you find us?"

"Well, I had just started my painting, when I saw an amazing sight. About twenty silver rabbits all hopping together towards the horizon. They were so beautiful – they looked like waves rippling on a shore."

"I wouldn't call them beautiful – more like annoying," said Timble.

"I thought what a lovely sketch I could draw if I could get close enough. They darted into a burrow and I climbed in behind them. I followed the tunnels deeper and deeper until I ended up here."

"And do you think you'll be able to find the way out again?" asked Stacey.

Moondoodle smiled. "Of course. But come and look in the room next door first."

Stacey, Timble, Zip and Zap all squeezed through the doorway into the next room. It was full of shelves, stacked with bottles of pop, fresh fruit, biscuits and picnic hampers.

Chapter 5

"Those naughty bunnies!" said Stacey. "They must have been pinching people's picnics for weeks."

"Here's our blanket," cried Zip and Zap together.

"I recognise this one too," said Timble, pointing to a stylish orange cool box. "Looks as though the bunnies might have visited Astro Pete."

"I don't think we will be able to carry that one as well as ours, do you?" said Stacey, laughing. "Come on, let's go and find a new picnic spot."

This time, the friends didn't leave their picnic unattended. They didn't feed any friendly-looking bunnies. Instead they ate until they were ready to pop.

Zip and Zap lay on their backs with their hands on their full tummies.

"I don't know if I'll fit through the door of the spaceship," said Zip.

"And if we do, we'll be too heavy to lift off the ground," said Zap.

"We'll just have to stay here all week," said Moondoodle.

Stacey leapt to her feet. "Anyone for a game of 'it'?"

Stacey started to chase Zip and Zap. Then Astro Pete, Jack Boom and Jill Zoom appeared, looking very sorry for themselves.

"You look worn out," said Timble.

Pete looked at the ground and murmured "Space bunnies... stole our lunch."

"We found ours in the end," said Timble. "We've just finished the jelly - it was very tasty."

"But we've got lots of other leftovers," said
Stacey, making room on the blanket. "Would
you like a carrot stick?"

The End

Book Bands for Guided Reading

Pink
Red
Yellow
Blue
Green
Orange
Turquoise
Purple
Gold
White

The Institute of Education book banding system is a scale of colours that reflects the various levels of reading difficulty. The bands are assigned by taking into account the content, the language style, the layout and phonics. Word, phrase and sentence level work is also taken into consideration.

Maverick Early Readers are a bright, attractive range of books covering the pink to white bands. All of these books have been book banded for guided reading to the industry standard and edited by a leading educational consultant.

To view the whole Maverick Readers scheme, visit our website at

www.maverickearlyreaders.com

Or scan the QR code above to view our scheme instantly!